Ready, Freddy! READER

SCHOLASTIC READER
LEVEL 2
250-750 WORDS

Halloween Parade

by ABBY KLEIN   illustrated by JOHN McKINLEY

SCHOLASTIC INC.
New York Toronto London Auckland Sydney
Mexico City New Delhi Hong Kong Buenos Aires

D0981328

To the students and families of
Franklin Elementary School,
who put on the best Halloween
carnival ever! Happy Halloween!
—A.K.

To Kendra, with love
—J.M.

ISBN-13: 978-0-545-14174-1
ISBN-10: 0-545-14174-5

Text copyright © 2009 by Abby Klein
Illustrations copyright © 2009 by John McKinley

12 11 10 9 8 7 6 5 4 3 2 1   9 10 11 12 13 14/0

Printed in the U.S.A.
First printing, September 2009

It was Halloween.

I wore my shark costume to school.

"What are you supposed to be?" asked Max.

"I am a hammerhead shark," I said.

"Cool," said Max.

Jessie had on a Dracula costume.

"You look cool," I said. "I like your fangs."

"I like your shark teeth."

"Those fangs are scary," said Chloe.

"Good," said Jessie. "I really want to win the prize for the scariest costume in the parade this year."

"Girls cannot dress up like Dracula," said Max.

"Yes, they can," said Jessie. "On Halloween you can be whatever you want to be."

"Well, I'm going to win the prize for the scariest this year," said Max. "My zombie costume is much scarier than your Dracula costume."

"Hey, everybody! Look at my costume," said Chloe.

She twirled all around the room.

"Isn't it beautiful?"

Chloe twirled right into a table.
She fell on the floor.
Her crown flew off her head.
"Oh, no!" Chloe cried. "My crown!
It's broken!"

Max started to laugh.

"That is not nice, Max," said Mrs. Wushy. "We need to help our friend Chloe."

"Now I can't win the prize for the prettiest costume," Chloe cried. Then she cried some more.

11

"I can help you fix your crown," said Jessie.

"You can?" said Chloe.

"Yes," said Jessie. "Give it to me. I have an idea."

Chloe gave Jessie the crown.

Jessie got some glue.
She glued the crown back together.

"There you go," said Jessie.
"Just like new."

She gave the crown to Chloe.

"Do not put it on yet," said Jessie.
"You have to let the glue dry."

"Thank you, Jessie," said Chloe.

"Jessie, you are a very good friend,"
said Mrs. Wushy.

"Okay, everybody," said Mrs. Wushy. "It's time to line up for the parade."

Chloe slowly put the sparkly crown on her head.

Then she got in line.

"I am ready now," she said. "The glue is all dry."

"Good," said Mrs. Wushy. "We have to get going. We do not want to be late for the parade."

"Let's go!" we all said.

We walked out the door to the playground.
All of the kids in the school were lining up
for the parade.

Our class got in line.

"Good morning, everyone," said our
principal. "The costume parade is about
to begin."

"Hooray!" we all cheered.

"Good luck!" said the principal.

He turned on some spooky Halloween
music, and we started to march.

I looked around at all the other kids.
There were some really cool costumes.

I started to laugh.

"What is so funny?" asked Robbie.

"That kid over there is dressed up like a hamburger!" I said.

Robbie looked over.

He started laughing, too!

"Look at that girl," said Jessie.
"She looks like a bunch of grapes!"
We all laughed some more.
We marched around the playground.
Then the music stopped.

"It is time to give out the prizes," said the principal.

Everyone sat down.

"There are so many great costumes this year. It was really hard to pick the winners."

"I hope I win a prize this year," said Jessie.

"You will," I said.

"What about me?" asked Chloe. "I want to win, too."

"The prize for the scariest costume
goes to the Dracula in Mrs. Wushy's class."
We all cheered.

"The prize for the most original costume
goes to the hammerhead shark, also in
Mrs. Wushy's class."

"That's not fair," said Chloe. "I want
to win a prize."

"The prize for the prettiest costume goes to…"

Chloe jumped up.

"Me!" yelled Chloe. "Me, me, me!"

Her crown came flying off her head again.

I caught it before it hit the ground.

"Good catch!" said Jessie.

We all laughed.

I put the crown back on Chloe's head.

"The prize goes to the princess in Mrs. Wushy's class," the principal announced.

Then we walked up to get our prizes.

We each got a little trophy with
a jack-o'-lantern on it.

"Thank you, Freddy and Jessie," said Chloe.

"Happy Halloween!" we said.

HAPPY HALLOWEEN!